SCOOBY-DOO!
and the
Pirate Treasure

W9-ATA-323

By Jean Lewis

Illustrated by William Lorencz and Michael Arens

 A GOLDEN BOOK • NEW YORK

Copyright © 2020 Hanna-Barbera.
SCOOBY-DOO and all related characters and elements
© & ™ Hanna-Barbera.
WB SHIELD: ™ & © WBEI. (s20)

Published in the United States by Golden Books, an imprint of Random House Children's Books, a division of Penguin Random House LLC, 1745 Broadway, New York, NY 10019, and in Canada by Penguin Random House Canada Limited, Toronto. Previously published in 1974 by Golden Press. Golden Books, A Golden Book, A Little Golden Book, the G colophon, and the distinctive gold spine are registered trademarks of Penguin Random House LLC.
rhcbooks.com
ISBN 978-0-593-17869-0 (trade) — ISBN 978-0-593-17870-6 (ebook)
Printed in the United States of America
10 9 8 7 6 5 4 3

"**S**low down, Fred," said Daphne. "We're nearly there. That sign says 'Pirate's Cove Dead Ahead.'"

"Even the sign sounds haunted!" muttered Shaggy.

Scooby-Doo shook under the backseat of the Mystery Machine.

"Shaggy!" Velma giggled. "You don't *really* believe the ghost of Captain Bones has come back for his long-lost pirate treasure! That's just a silly story."

"If it's not Captain Bones scaring folks away, then who is it?" asked Shaggy.

"That's what we're here to find out," said Fred, parking on the beach, "*after* we unload the food."

At the thought of a cookout, Shaggy cheered up and Scooby came out of hiding. The gang quickly built a cheery campfire.

Then Fred said, "Come on, Shaggy. We've got time for a quick look around before dark."

Reluctantly, Shaggy followed Fred, and Scooby
followed Shaggy. A little way down the beach,
they stopped to look at a tumbledown shack.
A For Sale sign hung on the door.

"Who'd buy this spooky house?" asked Shaggy.

"Captain Bones, maybe," Fred chuckled.

Suddenly, something swooped down toward Shaggy and Scoob.

"It's only a bat!" Fred yelled, but he was too late. They were already running to the van.

The two of them dived under the backseat and stayed there until the smell of grilling hamburgers brought them out. Much later—after seconds, thirds, and fourths—they began to feel better.

Scoob was snoozing beside the dying campfire, and Shaggy
was telling a ghost story, when suddenly a wild, rough voice
roared out of the darkness.

"Walk that plank, me hearties! Yo-ho-ho and a bottle of pop!"

Shaggy pointed at a shadowy figure beyond the firelight.
"Ye-ow! Look at that!"

Scooby saw the "ghost," and ran, howling, to the car.
Fred, Shaggy, Daphne, and Velma jumped to their feet.

"Don't let him get away!" Fred yelled.

Shaggy's teeth started to chatter.

"Look at that!" Fred pointed to the sand. "Footprints! No ghost ever leaves footprints. Come on—we'll go after him in the van!"

"Scoob and I'll stay here and guard the clues," Shaggy said.

As Fred and the girls drove off, Scooby seemed intent on a search of his own.

"Have another hamburger, Scoob?" said Shaggy, helping himself. But Scooby was too busy digging in the sand.

Shaggy grinned. "What've you got there, Captain Bones's pirate treasure?"

"R-r-ruff!" Scooby gave a bark of triumph, and up he came with a treasure of his own—a bone he had buried last summer. Shaggy kicked at the hole. *"Ouch!"* His toe hit something in the sand. "Look, Scoob!" he exclaimed. "It's an old sea chest!"

Scooby dropped his bone to help Shaggy dig. Finally, they
uncovered the lid of the chest, and Shaggy wrenched it open.
"It *is* Captain Bones's treasure!" he yelled.

The chest full of gold coins gleamed in the oncoming headlights
of the Mystery Machine—and the very first person to get out of
the van was the mysterious pirate himself!

Shaggy quickly shut the lid of the chest. "Mum's the word,"
he whispered to Scooby.

A few minutes later, the Mystery Inc. gang was sharing their cake with a very hungry pirate.

"Now," said Fred, "tell us who you really are and why you've been scaring everybody away from Pirate's Cove."

"Folks call me Cap'n Dan," said the ex-ghost. "I've been a sailor all my life. When I got too old for sailorin', I just wanted to settle down by the sea. But I didn't have enough money."

"So you 'haunted' that old beach shack by living in it," said Daphne.

Cap'n Dan nodded. "I figured the ghost of Captain Bones would keep folks away."

"Did you bury the captain's treasure, too?" Shaggy asked.

"What treasure?" asked Cap'n Dan.

"This treasure." Shaggy opened the chest.

Cap'n Dan gasped. "Why, there's enough gold there to buy
a hundred houses!"

Mystery Inc. shared a look.

"Cap'n Dan," Fred said, "we want you to have a share of the treasure. If it hadn't been for you, the gold might never have been found."

Meanwhile, Velma thought of something the gang could do with their share of the gold.

The gang got busy, and all the rest of the summer, they took kids—ones who had never had a day of beach fun—to Pirate's Cove in the Mystery Machine!

They swam and surfed, they heard Cap'n Dan's
exciting sea stories—and they ate delicious cookouts
served by Mystery, Inc.

Best of all, each day when the sea chest was opened, there were enough chocolate doubloons and licorice pieces of eight in it for all the visitors at Pirate's Cove!